HANS CHRISTIAN
ANDERSEN'S
FAIRY TALES

SELECTED AND ILLUSTRATED
BY LISBETH ZWERGER
TRANSLATED
BY ANTHEA BELL

A Michael Neugebauer Book
NORTH-SOUTH BOOKS / NEW YORK / LONDON

CONTENTS

The Sandman · 5

The Jumpers · 25

Thumbeline · 29

The Tinderbox · 45

The Rose Tree Regiment · 55

The Naughty Boy · 59

The Swineherd · 63

The Emperor's New Clothes · 73

The Princess and the Pea · 79

The Nightingale · 83

The Little Match Girl · 99

No one in the world knows as many stories as the Sandman. Yes, indeed, he tells really wonderful stories!

The Sandman comes in the evening, when children are sitting at the table, or perhaps on their stools. He comes upstairs very quietly in his stocking feet, opens the door softly, and then he sprinkles the finest of sand into their eyes. They don't see him, because they can hardly keep their eyes open. He creeps quietly up behind them, blows gently on their necks, and they begin to feel sleepy. The Sandman does them no harm, for he is kind to children. He just wants them to be quiet, and they are more likely to be quiet once they have been put to bed. He wants them to be quiet so that he can tell them stories.

Once the children are asleep, the Sandman sits on their beds. He wears lovely clothes and a silk coat, but what color it is I cannot say, for it looks green, red, or blue depending which way he turns. He has an umbrella under each arm. One has pictures on it, and he holds it over good children to make them dream of wonderful things all night long. The other has no pictures on it at all. He holds that one over naughty children, and then they sleep heavily and have had no dreams at all when they wake in the morning.

Well, now let's hear the stories the Sandman once told a little boy named Hjalmar. He came to see Hjalmar every day for a week, and told him some very fine stories, seven of them altogether, because there are seven days in a week.

THE SANDMAN

MONDAY

"Now then," said the Sandman one evening, when he had put Hjalmar to bed, "I'm going to make your room look pretty." And all the flowers in their pots grew and became tall trees with long branches that went all along the ceiling and down the walls, so that the whole room looked like a beautiful bower. The branches were covered with flowers, and every one of them was even lovelier than a rose. They were wonderfully fragrant too, and if you ate one it tasted sweeter than jam. Golden fruit gleamed among the branches, and buns full of raisins hung on them too. It was a wonderful sight. But then a pitiful wailing was heard coming from the drawer of the table where Hjalmar had put his schoolbooks.

"What's all this?" asked the Sandman, and he went to the table and opened the drawer. It was Hjalmar's slate making the noise! One of the figures in the sum on it was wrong, and all the others were pushing and shoving until the whole slate was in danger of falling to bits. The slate pencil was leaping and jumping about like a little dog on the end of its string, trying to help correct the sum, but it couldn't. More wailing came from Hjalmar's exercise book—it was a really miserable sound. Each page had a capital letter and a small letter written on it, as examples to be copied out in rows. Other letters stood next to these handsome ones and thought they looked the same, but they were the letters Hjalmar had written, and they were lying about all over the place, as if they had fallen over the penciled line instead of standing on it properly.

"Look, this is the way to stand!" said the handsome copybook letters. "You want to slope this way, with a nice flourish to you!"

"We only wish we could," said the letters Hjalmar had written, "but we feel so poorly! We can't!"

"Then you'd better have some medicine to make you better," said the Sandman.

"No, no!" cried the letters, standing up straight at once.

"Well, I can see we won't get any stories told this evening," said the Sandman. "I'd better drill these letters. One, two! One, two!" he shouted, drilling the letters until they stood up as straight and handsome as copybook letters can.

However, when Hjalmar looked at them in the morning after the Sandman had left, they were just as bad as ever.

TUESDAY

As soon as Hjalmar was in bed the Sandman touched all the furniture in the room with his little magic wand, and at once it began to talk. All the pieces of furniture were talking about themselves, except for the spittoon, which kept silent. He wished they wouldn't be so vain, chattering on and on about themselves with never a thought for him. He just stood humbly in the corner letting people spit in him. There was a big picture in a gilded frame hanging over the chest of drawers. It was a landscape, a picture showing tall old trees, flowers in the grass, and a great river winding its way through the forest, passing many castles on its way to the open sea. The Sandman turned his magic wand on the painting, and the birds in the picture began to sing, the branches of the trees swayed, and the clouds moved across the sky. You could see their shadows passing over the landscape.

Then the Sandman lifted little Hjalmar up to the frame, and he climbed right into the picture and stood there in the tall grass. The sun was shining down on him through the branches of the trees. He ran to the river and climbed into a little boat moored there. It was painted red and white, with sails shining like silver. Six swans, all with golden crowns around their necks and bright blue stars on their heads, drew the boat past the green woods where trees told tales of robbers and witches, and the flowers talked about the pretty little elves and the stories they had heard from butterflies.

Beautiful fish with scales like gold and silver swam after the boat. Every now and then they jumped, and there was a splash in the water. Long lines of red-and-blue birds, both large and small, flew after them. Midges danced in the air, and the cockchafer boomed. They all wanted to follow Hjalmar, and they all had stories to tell. What a boating trip that was! Sometimes the woods were thick and dark, sometimes they were like a lovely garden full of sunshine and flowers, with great castles of glass and marble among them. Princesses stood on the castle balconies, and they were all little girls Hjalmar knew well and used to play with. They stretched out their hands, holding the nicest sugar pigs you could buy, and Hjalmar took one end of each sugar pig as he sailed past while the princess held tight to the other, so that each had a bit of it. The princess had the smaller half of the sugar pig and Hjalmar had the

larger half! Little princes stood on guard outside every castle, shouldering their golden swords and throwing raisins and tin soldiers. They were real princes and no mistake! Hjalmar sailed on, and the boat seemed to pass sometimes through woods, sometimes through great halls or a town. He sailed through the town where the nurse who used to look after him when he was a baby lived. She loved him very much. She nodded and waved and sang a little song she had made up herself and sent him:

> *I often think of you, dear child,*
> *My darling little boy!*
> *To kiss your mouth, your brow so mild,*
> *Your cheeks was all my joy.*
> *I heard your first words, shared your mirth,*
> *But then we had to part.*
> *May God protect you here on earth,*
> *The angel of my heart.*

The birds all sang too, and the flowers danced on their stalks, and the old trees nodded as if the Sandman were telling them stories as well.

WEDNESDAY

The rain was pouring down outside in torrents. Hjalmar could hear it even in his sleep, and when the Sandman opened the window, there was water up to the sill. The floods were like a lake outside, and a splendid ship was moored close to the house. "Would you like to come sailing, little Hjalmar?" asked the Sandman. "You can travel to foreign lands tonight and be back again in the morning."

All at once Hjalmar was on the wonderful ship, dressed in his Sunday best, and immediately the weather cleared. They sailed down the streets, cruised around the church, and soon they were out on the high seas. They sailed so far that they couldn't see the shore anymore, and then they saw a flock of storks flying from land on their way to the warm countries. The storks flew in single file, and they had all come a very long way. One of them was so tired that his wings could hardly carry him anymore. He was the last in line, and soon he was lagging far behind the others. At last he sank lower and lower, with outstretched wings. He beat his wings once or twice more, but it was no good. His feet touched the ship's rigging, he fell down past the sail, and he landed on the deck. The cabin boy picked him up and put him in the henhouse, with the hens and ducks and turkeys. The poor stork stood among them feeling very downcast.

"Look at that funny bird!" said the hens.

And the turkey puffed himself up as big as he could and asked the stork his name, while the ducks waddled about, nudging each other and going, "Quack! Quack!" The stork told them about the hot lands of Africa and the pyramids and the ostrich who runs about the desert like a wild horse, but the ducks couldn't understand a word he said. They just nudged each other again, quacking, "Isn't he silly? Isn't he silly?"

"He certainly is!" gobbled the turkey. The stork said nothing, but he thought about Africa.

"You have an elegant pair of long legs there!" said the turkey. "What did they cost you a yard?"

"Quack, quack, quack!" went the ducks, giggling, but the stork looked as if he hadn't heard.

"Well, you might have joined in the laughter!" said the turkey. "I mean, it was very funny! Or perhaps it was beneath your notice? Can't take a joke, I see! Well, let's go on amusing ourselves!" And the hens clucked and the ducks quacked, thinking themselves extremely witty.

But Hjalmar went over to the henhouse, opened the door, and called the stork, who hopped out on deck. He was feeling rested now and nodded to Hjalmar as if to thank him. Then he spread his wings and flew away to the hot countries, while the hens clucked, the ducks quacked, and the turkey went bright red in the face.

"Watch out, or we'll make you into soup tomorrow!" said Hjalmar, and the next moment he woke up in his own little bed. What a wonderful voyage the Sandman had sent him on that night!

THURSDAY

"Now," said the Sandman, "don't be afraid, and I'll show you a little mouse!" He held out his hand, with the pretty little creature in it. "She's come to invite you to a wedding," he said. "Two mice are getting married tonight. They live under your mother's dining room floor, and I believe they have a very nice mouse hole there."

"But how can I get into a little mouse hole under the floor?" asked Hjalmar.

"Leave that to me!" said the Sandman. "I'll shrink you!" And he touched Hjalmar with his magic wand. Hjalmar immediately shrank, becoming smaller and smaller until he was no bigger than a finger. "You can borrow the tin soldier's clothes. I think they'll fit you, and a uniform looks well at a party!"

"Oh yes!" said Hjalmar, and in a moment he was dressed like a smart tin soldier.

"Will you be so good as to sit in your mother's thimble?" said the little mouse. "Then I can have the pleasure of pulling you along!"

"How kind of you to go to so much trouble, ma'am!" said Hjalmar, and they drove off to the mouse wedding.

First of all they went down a long passage under the floor, only just big enough for the thimble to get through it. The whole passage was lighted by burning torches made of bits of rotten wood.

"Doesn't it smell nice down here?" said the mouse, who was pulling Hjalmar along in the thimble. "The whole passage has been carpeted with bacon rind. What could be better?"

Then they came into the room where the wedding was to be held. All the little lady mice stood on the right, whispering as if they were making fun of one another. All the gentlemen mice stood on the left, stroking their whiskers with their paws. And the happy couple were in the middle of the room, standing on a scooped-out cheese rind and kissing each other lovingly in front of the whole company, because they were already engaged and now they were about to be married.

More guests kept arriving. The mice were in danger of trampling one another, and the bridal couple had placed themselves in the doorway so that you could get neither in nor out. The whole room had been carpeted with bacon rind, like the passage, and that was all there was to eat, except for a pea, which was the wedding cake. A little

mouse who was a member of the family had nibbled the happy couple's names in it, or rather their initials, so that made it very special.

All the mice said it was a wonderful wedding, and they had found the conversation most entertaining.

Then Hjalmar rode home. He felt he had certainly been to a very grand party, even if it meant shrinking to a size where he could wear the tin soldier's uniform.

FRIDAY

"You wouldn't believe how many grown-up people would like to get their hands on me," said the Sandman. "Especially people who have done something bad. 'Dear Sandman,' they say, 'we can't get a wink of sleep, we lie awake all night seeing our evil deeds sitting on the bed like ugly little gnomes, sprinkling hot water over us. Please come and drive them away so that we can get some sleep!' Then they sigh deeply, and say, 'We'll be happy to pay you. Good night, Sandman! You'll find the money on the windowsill.' But I don't offer such things for money," said the Sandman.

"What are we going to do tonight?" asked Hjalmar.

"Well, I wonder if you'd like to go to another wedding? It won't be the same as last night's. Your sister's big boy doll, Herman, is going to marry the other doll, Bertha. It's the doll's birthday too, so there will be lots of presents."

"I know!" said Hjalmar. "Whenever the dolls need new clothes my sister gives either a birthday party or a wedding for them. They must have had about a hundred weddings!"

"Yes, but tonight is the hundred and first, and after a hundred and one they can't get married anymore, so tonight's will be a very fine wedding indeed," said the Sandman. "Look over there!"

Hjalmar looked at the table and saw that there were lights in the windows of the little cardboard dollhouse, while all the tin soldiers were presenting arms outside it. The bride and groom were sitting on the floor, leaning on the table leg and looking very thoughtful—no doubt for good reasons. But the Sandman, wearing Grandmother's black blouse as a gown, married them. When the marriage ceremony was over, all the furniture in the room struck up the following beautiful song. It had been written by the pencil, and had a tune that was like the rat-a-tat-tat of drums.

> Our song will travel like the wind
> And the bride and groom at home will find.
> Their heads are held high, they're of noble kind,
> All made of leather and most refined.
> Three cheers for the couple let us remind
> You all to give, come weather, come wind.

Then it was time for the wedding presents. The dolls had asked their friends not to give them anything to eat, because they were in love, and they could live on love. "Shall we go into the country or travel abroad for our honeymoon?" asked the bridegroom.

They turned for advice to the swallow, who had traveled widely, and the old hen who had hatched out five broods of chicks. The swallow told them about the beautiful warm lands where bunches of grapes hang huge and heavy, where the air is mild, and the mountains are tinged with colors never seen here.

"But they don't have cabbages there!" said the hen. "I spent a summer in the country with my chicks, and there was a gravel pit where we could go and scratch about. We could get into a garden where cabbages grew too. They were lovely green cabbages! I can't imagine anything nicer."

"One cabbage stalk looks exactly like the next, if you ask me," said the swallow, and the weather here is often so bad!"

"You get used to it," said the hen.

"But it's cold here. There are frosts!"

"They're good for the cabbages," said the hen. "Anyway, we sometimes get warm weather too. Didn't we have a summer four years ago that went on for five whole weeks, and it was so hot you could hardly breathe? And we don't get all those nasty poisonous creatures you find abroad. There are no robbers here either. Anyone who doesn't think our country the finest in the world is a rotten scoundrel and doesn't deserve to be here at all," said the hen, bursting into tears. "I've traveled too, you know! I've been all of twelve miles in a coop! Traveling is no fun at all, I can assure you!"

"That hen is talking sense!" said the doll Bertha. "I'd rather not go mountaineering either. Up one side and down another! No, let's go to the gravel pit and walk in the garden where the cabbages grow."

And that was what they did.

SATURDAY

"Are you going to tell me a story?" asked little Hjalmar as soon as the Sandman had put him to bed.

"We won't have time for stories this evening," said the Sandman, holding his pretty umbrella over him. "Look at these Chinese people!" And, indeed, the whole umbrella looked like a Chinese bowl, with blue trees and pointed bridges with little Chinese people standing on them and nodding their heads. "We must have the whole world spick and span for tomorrow," said the Sandman, "because tomorrow is Sunday, and that's a holy day. I must go over to the church tower to see if the little brownies who live there are shining up the bells to make them ring well. I must go out to the fields to see if the wind is blowing the dust off the grass and leaves. And most important of all, I must take all the stars down and polish them! I'll collect them in my apron, but they must be numbered first, and so must their holes in the sky, so that they can go back into their proper places, or they won't stay put and we shall have too many shooting stars falling one after another!"

"Now you listen to me, Mr. Sandman," said an old portrait, which hung on the wall near Hjalmar's bed. "I'm Hjalmar's great-grandfather, and I'd like to thank you for telling the lad stories, but you mustn't confuse him! Stars cannot be taken down and polished! Stars are heavenly bodies like the earth, and that's the beauty of them!"

"Thank you, old great-grandfather," said the Sandman. "Thank you very much. You are the head of the family, and a very old head indeed! But I'm even older, you know. I'm an old heathen, and I was known to the Greeks and Romans as the god of dreams. I've been in the grandest of houses, and I go there still. I know how to deal with both great and small. Very well, you can have your say now!"

"I see a person isn't even allowed to speak his mind these days!" said the old portrait. And with that Hjalmar woke up.

SUNDAY

"Good evening," said the Sandman, and Hjalmar nodded, jumping up to turn his great-grandfather's portrait to the wall so that it wouldn't interrupt the way it had interrupted yesterday.

"Now, tell me some stories!" he said. "Tell me the story about the five green peas who lived in one pod, and the one about the frog who would a-wooing go, and the one about the darning needle who thought herself so fine that she imagined she was a sewing needle!"

"You can have too much of a good thing," said the Sandman. "I want to show you something else tonight. I'm going to show you my brother. He is a sandman too, but he never visits anyone more than once, and then he takes that person up on his horse and tells him stories. He knows only two stories, one more wonderful than anyone in the world can imagine, and one so terrible that—well, there's no describing it!" And the Sandman lifted little Hjalmar up to the window and said, "Look, there's my brother, the other sandman. He is also called Death. You see, he isn't as frightening as they paint him in picture books, where he's nothing but bones. No, he has silver braid on his coat and wears a very fine military uniform, with a black velvet cape flying out behind him and his horse. See how he gallops along!"

And Hjalmar watched the other sandman ride by, taking people both young and old upon his horse. He put some of them in front of him and some of them behind him, but first he asked what their reports were like. They all said they had good reports.

"Well, let me see for myself," said he, and so they had to show him their reports. All the people with "Very good" or "Outstanding" on their reports were placed in front of Death on the horse, and heard the beautiful story, but those who had reports saying "Moderate" or "Poor" were placed behind Death and had to listen to the terrible story. They trembled and wept and tried to jump off the horse, but they couldn't: it was as if they were stuck fast to it.

"I think Death is the best sandman of all," said Hjalmar. "I'm not afraid of him."

"And I hope you never will be!" said the Sandman. "Just make sure you get a good report!"

"Very educational!" muttered great-grandfather's portrait. "Well, a person should be

allowed to speak his mind. It comes in useful." And he was satisfied.

Those are the stories the Sandman told Hjalmar, and perhaps he will tell you some more himself tonight.

THE JUMPERS

Once upon a time the flea, the grasshopper, and the jumping jack wanted to find out which of them could jump the highest, and they invited the world and his wife to see the show. When the three of them were in the room together, you could tell that they were all really good at jumping.

"I'll give my daughter to whomever jumps highest!" said the king. "It would be a shame for them to jump for nothing!"

The flea came forward first. He had elegant manners and nodded to all present, for he had noble blood in him and was accustomed to mixing in human society, and that meant a good deal.

Next came the grasshopper, who was considerably stouter, but looked very fine in the green uniform he wore. Moreover, he said he came of a very old family in the land of Egypt, and was highly thought of over here as well. He came from the fields, and now he lived in a house of cards three stories high. The cards used to build it showed the kings and knaves, with the colored pictures on the inside, and the doors and windows were cut out of cards showing the queen of hearts. "I sing so well," said he, "that sixteen native crickets who have chirped from youth, but don't live in a house of cards, have been so annoyed by hearing me that they became even thinner than they were before!"

Both the flea and the grasshopper spoke highly of their own talents, and said they thought they were fit to marry a princess.

As for the jumping jack, he said nothing, but folks believed that meant he was thinking all the harder, and when the court dog sniffed him he said he was sure the jumping jack came from a good family. The old councillor, who had been given three decorations for keeping silent, said that he saw the jumping jack had the gift of prophecy: you could tell from his back whether it was going to be a mild winter or a harsh one, which is more than you can tell from the back of the man who writes the almanac.

"Well, I won't say anything!" said the old king. "But I can think what I like!"

Now it was time for the jumping to begin. The flea jumped so high that no one could see him, so they said he hadn't jumped at all, and he was cheating.

The grasshopper jumped only half as high as the flea, but he jumped right in the king's face, and the king said that was nasty.

The jumping jack stood there silent for some time, thinking the matter over, until people thought he couldn't jump at all.

"I hope he doesn't feel sick!" said the court dog, sniffing him again. *Whoosh!* The jumping jack gave a little leap and landed in the lap of the princess, who was sitting on a low golden stool.

Then the king said, "The highest jump was the jump up to my daughter, for you can't go any higher. But it took a quick wit to find that out, and the jumping jack is clever and has brains."

So he had won the princess.

"But I jumped highest!" said the flea. "Still, it comes to the same thing! Let her have the jumping jack for all I care! I jumped the highest, but it seems that looks are all that count in this world!"

So the flea went abroad on active service, and they say that he was killed.

The grasshopper went and sat down in the ditch and thought about the way of the world, and he agreed: "Looks are all that count! Looks are all that count!" And so he sang his own sad song, and I wrote this story about it. You needn't believe every word, even though you've seen it in print.

THUMBELINE

Once upon a time there was a woman who longed to have a tiny child of her own, but she had no idea where to get one. So she went to see an old witch, and asked her, "I do so long to have a little child; won't you tell me where I can get one?"

"Oh, we'll soon deal with that," said the witch. "Here, take this barleycorn. It is no ordinary barleycorn, not the kind that grows in the farmer's fields or is given to the chickens to eat! Put it in a flowerpot, and you will see what you will see!"

"Thank you kindly," said the woman, and she gave the witch some money. Then she went home and planted the barleycorn, and it instantly grew into a large and beautiful flower. The flower looked just like a tulip, but its petals were tightly furled as if it were still in bud.

"What a lovely flower!" said the woman, and she kissed its beautiful red-and-yellow petals. But the moment that she kissed it, the flower burst open with a loud snap. Anyone could see it really was a tulip, but there was a tiny little girl, very delicate and sweet, sitting in the middle of the flower on its green center. She was no bigger than your thumb, and so she was called Thumbeline.

She was given a prettily lacquered walnut shell for a cradle, and she lay there on blue violet petals, with a rose petal coverlet over her. She slept in her cradle by night, but by day she played on the table. The woman had put a plate on the table, holding a wreath of flowers with their stalks hanging down in the water and a big tulip petal floating on top of it. Thumbeline could ferry herself from one side of the plate to the other on this petal, using two white horsehairs for oars. It was a pretty sight. She could sing too, in the sweetest, loveliest voice that ever was heard.

One night as she lay in her pretty little bed, an ugly toad came hopping in through the window, which had a broken pane. The toad was big and ugly and wet. She hopped right over to the table where Thumbeline lay asleep under her red rose petal.

"What a nice wife she would make for my son!" said the toad. And she picked up the walnut shell where Thumbeline lay asleep, and hopped away with it, right through the broken pane and out into the garden.

There was a big, broad stream running by. Its banks were all muddy and marshy, and the toad lived here with her son. Oh, dear, he was so ugly and nasty, and he looked just like his mother!

All he could say when he saw the sweet little girl in her walnut shell was, "Croak! Croak! Croak, croak, croak!"

"Don't speak so loud, or you'll wake her," said the old mother toad. "She could still run away from us, for she's as light as swansdown. We will lay her on one of the big water-lily leaves on the stream. Little and light as she is, it will be like an island to her! Then she won't be able to run away from us while we clear out our best room down in the mud, where the pair of you are to keep house!"

There were a great many water lilies growing out in the stream, with broad green leaves that looked as if they were floating on top of the water. The leaf that was farthest away was the biggest one too. The old mother toad swam out to this leaf and placed Thumbeline in her walnut shell on it.

The poor little thing woke up very early the next morning, and when she saw where she was, she began to weep bitterly, for there was water all around the big green leaf and she could not get to land at all.

The old toad was down in the mud, decking out her best room with reeds and yellow marsh-marigold petals to make it pretty for her new daughter-in-law. Then she and her ugly son swam out to the leaf where Thumbeline lay. They were going to fetch her pretty bed and put it in the bridal chamber before she came over herself. The old mother toad curtsied low in the water to her, and said: "This is my son, who is to be your husband, and the two of you will live very comfortably together down in the mud!"

"Croak! Croak! Croak, croak, croak!" was all her son could find to say.

So then she picked up the pretty little bed and swam away with it. Thumbeline sat all alone on the green leaf, weeping because she did not want to live with the nasty toad or be married to her ugly son. The little fish swimming down in the water must have seen the toad and heard what she said, for they put their heads out to see the little girl for themselves. As soon as they set eyes on her, they loved her so much that they would have been very sorry to see her forced to go down and live with the ugly toad! No, that must never be! They clustered together in the water around the green stalk of the leaf on which she was sitting and nibbled through it with their teeth. Then the leaf with Thumbeline floated downstream far, far away, where the toad could not

follow. Thumbeline floated past a great many places, and the little birds perching in the bushes saw her and sang, "Oh, what a lovely little lady!" The leaf floated on and on with her, and so Thumbeline came to another country.

A pretty little white butterfly kept flying around Thumbeline and at last settled on the leaf, for it had taken a liking to the little girl. Thumbeline was very happy now. The toads could no longer get at her, and they were passing such pretty scenery. The sun shone on the water like glimmering gold, and as the leaf sped along even faster, Thumbeline took her sash and tied one end to the butterfly and the other to the leaf.

At that moment a big June beetle came flying up and saw her. He immediately clasped her slender waist with his claws and flew up into a tree with her.

But the green leaf floated on downstream, taking the butterfly with it, for the butterfly was tied to the leaf and could not get away.

Oh, dear, how frightened poor Thumbeline was when the June beetle flew up into the tree with her. She was saddest of all because of the pretty white butterfly she had tied to the leaf; if it could not get free now, it would starve to death! But the June beetle didn't care about that. He settled on the biggest green leaf in the tree with her, gave her nectar from the flowers to eat, and said she was very pretty, even if she was not in the least like a June beetle. Then all the other June beetles who lived in that tree came visiting. They looked at Thumbeline, and the June beetle girls shrugged their feelers and said, "Why, she has only two legs—what a wretched sight!"

"Oh, she has no feelers!" they said. "And her waist is so slim! She looks just like a human being. How ugly she is!" said all the lady June beetles, and yet Thumbeline was very pretty indeed. Or so the June beetle who had caught her thought; but when all the others said she was ugly he ended up believing them, and did not want her anymore, so now she could go where she liked. They flew down from the tree with her and put her on a daisy. She cried, because she was so ugly that the June beetles didn't want anything to do with her—and yet she was the prettiest thing you ever saw, as fine and bright as the loveliest of rose petals.

All summer long poor Thumbeline lived alone in the great wood. She wove herself a bed of grass blades and slung it under a big burdock leaf, so that the rain could not get at her; she squeezed nectar from the flowers and ate it, and she drank the dew that stood on the leaves every morning. So summer and autumn passed by, but then winter came, and the winter was long and cold. All the birds who had sung so beautifully for her flew away. The trees and the flowers faded, the big burdock leaf under which she had slept curled up and became a yellow, withered stem, and she was terribly cold, for her clothes were worn out. Poor little Thumbeline was so tiny and delicate that she was in danger of freezing to death. It began to snow, and every snowflake that fell on her was like a whole shovelful being thrown on one of us, since we are big folk, and she was only the size of your thumb. So she wrapped herself in a dead leaf, but there was no warmth in it, and she shivered with the cold. Beyond the wood to which she had come there lay a big wheat field, but the wheat had been cut long ago, and there was only bare, dry stubble on the frozen ground. The stubble was like a forest to Thumbeline as she walked through it, trembling dreadfully with cold. At last she came to a field mouse's door, a little hole down among the stubble. The field mouse was very warm and comfortable living down there, with a whole room full of grain and a fine kitchen and a larder. Poor Thumbeline stood at her door like a beggar girl, asking for a tiny piece of barleycorn, because she had had nothing at all to eat for two days.

"You poor little thing!" said the field mouse, who was a good old creature at heart. "Come into my nice warm room and share my meal!" She took a fancy to Thumbeline, and told her, "You can stay the winter with me if you like, but you must keep my house clean and tell me stories. I'm very fond of stories." So Thumbeline did as the good old field mouse asked, and she was very comfortable indeed.

"We'll soon be having a visitor," said the field mouse. "My neighbor usually comes to visit me every day of the week. He is even better off than me, and has a finer house than mine, with great big rooms to live in, and he wears a fine black velvet fur coat. If you could only marry him, you'd be well provided for. But he can't see, so you must tell him the very best stories you know!"

However, Thumbeline did not like this idea. She didn't want to marry the neighbor a bit, for he was a mole.

And so he came visiting in his black velvet coat. The field mouse said he was very rich and very clever, and his property was over twenty times bigger than hers. The mole knew all sorts of things, but he could not bear the sun and the pretty flowers, and he never spoke well of them because he had never seen them. Thumbeline had to sing for him, so she sang "Ladybird, ladybird, fly away home," and "The monk in the meadow." The mole fell in love with her for her pretty voice, but he said nothing yet, for he was a very cautious man.

Recently he had dug a long passage through the earth from his house to the field mouse's, and he said the field mouse and Thumbeline could walk there whenever they liked. He told them not to be afraid of the dead bird lying in the passage. The bird was a whole one, with beak and feathers and all; it could only just have died when winter came, and now it lay buried on the spot where he had dug his own passage.

The mole took a piece of rotten wood in his mouth, for rotten wood shines like fire in the dark, and went ahead to light the way down the long, dark passage for them. When they came to the place where the dead bird lay, the mole put his big nose against the roof and pushed up the earth, making a large hole so that the light could shine in. In the middle of the floor lay a dead swallow, its beautiful wings close to its sides, its legs and head tucked into its feathers. Poor bird, it must surely have died of cold. Thumbeline felt very sorry for it, for she loved all the little birds dearly. They had sung and chirped for her so prettily all summer long. But the mole gave it a kick with his stumpy leg and said, "That's the end of all his twittering! How miserable to be born a bird! Thank heaven none of my own children will be birds—all a bird can do is sing, and then starve to death in the winter."

"You are a sensible man, and you may well say so," agreed the field mouse.

"What reward does a bird get for its singing when winter comes? It must starve and freeze, and yet birds are thought so wonderful!"

Thumbeline said nothing, but when the other two had turned their backs on the bird she bent down, parted the feathers over its head and kissed its closed eyes.

Perhaps this was the very bird that sang so beautifully for me in summer, she thought. How happy the dear, pretty bird made me then!

The mole stopped up the hole through which daylight shone in and took the ladies home again. That night, however, Thumbeline could not sleep. She made a beautiful

big blanket out of hay, carried it down and wrapped it around the pretty bird. She tucked some soft cotton she had found in the field mouse's house close to the bird's sides, to make him a warm place to lie in the cold earth.

"Good-bye, you lovely little bird!" she said. "Good-bye, and thank you for your beautiful songs in summer, when all the trees were green and the sun shone so warmly!" And she laid her head on the bird's breast; but then she had a shock, for it felt as if something were beating inside. It was the bird's heart! The swallow was not dead, only unconscious, and now that he was warmer, he was coming back to life.

Swallows all fly to the warm countries in autumn, but if one of them lingers too long it freezes, falls to the ground and lies where it has fallen as if dead, and the cold snow covers it up.

Thumbeline was trembling with fright, for as she was only the size of your thumb, the bird looked gigantic to her. But she plucked up her courage, tucked the cotton closer around the poor swallow, and fetched a mint leaf she herself had been using as a coverlet to lay over the bird's head.

Next night she slipped down to see him again. He was awake, but so tired he could only open his eyes for a moment, to see Thumbeline standing there with a piece of rotten wood in her hand, since she had no other lantern.

"Thank you, my dear sweet child, thank you!" said the sick swallow. "I am so nice and warm now! I'll soon have my strength back, and then I'll be able to fly out into the warm sunshine again!"

"Oh, but it's so cold outside now!" she said. "It is snowing and freezing! You must stay warm in bed, and I'll look after you!"

She brought the swallow water in a flower petal. He drank it and told her he had hurt a wing on a thorn bush, so that he could not fly as fast as the other swallows when they all went far, far away to the warm countries. At last he had fallen to the ground, and that was all he knew. He had no idea how he had come to be under the ground.

So he stayed down there all winter, and Thumbeline was good to him, and loved him very much. She did not let the mole or the field mouse know anything about it, because they would not care about helping the poor sick swallow.

As soon as spring came, and the sun's rays warmed the earth, the swallow said good-bye to Thumbeline. She opened up the hole the mole had made in the roof overhead. The sun shone in on them so beautifully, and the swallow asked if she would like to come with him. He said she could sit on his back, and they would fly far away into the green wood. But Thumbeline knew it would hurt the old field mouse's feelings if she left like that.

"No," said Thumbeline, "I can't go."

"Good-bye, good-bye, you sweet, good girl," said the swallow, and he flew out into the sunshine. Thumbeline watched him go, and tears came to her eyes, because she loved the poor swallow so much.

"Tweet! Tweet!" sang the bird, and he flew away into the green wood.

Thumbeline was very sad. She was not allowed to go out into the warm sunlight. The seed corn sown in the field above the mouse hole was growing tall now, and it was like a thick forest to a poor little girl only as big as your thumb.

"You must spend the summer sewing your trousseau!" the field mouse told her, for neighbor Mole, who was so tedious but had a black velvet fur coat, had asked for her hand in marriage. "You will have both wool and linen to wear, and underclothes and household linen, when you are married to the mole."

So Thumbeline had to sit at the distaff and spin, and the field mouse hired four spiders to come too, and spin and weave by day and by night. Every evening the mole came visiting, and he always said that when the summer came to an end, and the sun was not as hot as it was now, when it baked the earth as hard as stone—yes, when summer was over, his wedding to Thumbeline would be held. She did not like the thought of it at all, for she could not bear the tedious mole. Every morning at sunrise, and every evening at sunset, she would slip outside the door, and when the wind blew the ears of wheat apart so that she could see the blue sky, she thought how bright and lovely it was out here, and longed to see her old friend the swallow again. But the swallow did not come back. He had flown far away into the beautiful green wood.

When autumn came Thumbeline had her trousseau ready. "You are to be married in four weeks' time," the field mouse told her.

But Thumbeline wept and said she did not want to marry the tiresome old mole.
"Fiddle-de-dee!" said the field mouse. "Don't be so stubborn, or I'll bite you with my white teeth! It's a very fine husband you are getting! Why, the queen herself does not own a black velvet fur coat the like of his. He has stores in his kitchen and his cellar, and you ought to thank heaven for him!"

So the wedding was to take place. The mole had already come to fetch Thumbeline away to live with him deep down underground. They would never again come out to see the warm sun, for the mole could not stand sunshine. Poor child, she was very unhappy to have to say good-bye to the beautiful sun. While she was living with the field mouse she had at least been able to step outside the door and see it.

"Good-bye, bright sun!" she said, stretching her arms up into the air, and she walked a little way beyond the field mouse's hole, for the wheat had been reaped now and there was nothing left but dry stubble. "Good-bye, good-bye!" she said, putting her arms around a little red flower that grew there. "Give my love to my dear swallow, if you see him!"

"Tweet! Tweet!" sang a voice overhead at that very moment. She looked up, and it was the swallow flying by. He was delighted to see Thumbeline. She told him how little she liked the thought of marrying the ugly mole and going to live underground where the sun never shone. She had to shed tears—she could not help it.

"The cold winter is coming," said the swallow. "I'm flying away to the warm countries. Would you like to come with me? You can sit on my back. Just tie yourself on with your sash, and we'll fly away from the ugly mole and his dark house, far away over the mountains to the warm countries, where the sun shines more beautifully than it does here, and where it is always summer and there are lovely flowers. Do fly away with me, dear little Thumbeline who saved my life when I lay frozen in the dark underground!"

"Oh yes, I'll come with you!" said Thumbeline, and she sat on the bird's back, with her feet on his outspread wings, and tied her sash to one of his strongest feathers. Then the swallow flew high up into the air, over the woods and over the water, over the high mountains where snow lies all the year round. Thumbeline was freezing in the cold air, but she crept in among the bird's warm feathers, and just put her little

head out to see all the wonders down below. So they came to the warm countries. The sun shone much more brightly there than it does here, the sky was twice as high, and the most beautiful green and blue grapes grew all along the ditches and the hedges. The woods were full of oranges and lemons, the air was fragrant with myrtle and mint, and the prettiest of children ran down the road playing with big, bright butterflies.

But still the swallow flew on, and everything became even more beautiful. A shining white marble castle of the olden days stood beneath splendid green trees, by the side of a blue lake. Vines clambered around its tall columns, and there were a great many swallows' nests up at the top. One of them belonged to the swallow who was carrying Thumbeline.

"Here is my home," said the swallow. "But if you'd like to choose one of the magnificent flowers growing down below for yourself, I'll put you into it, and you will live there as comfortably as ever you could wish!"

"Oh, that would be wonderful!" she said, clapping her little hands.

One big white marble column had fallen to the ground and was broken into three, but the loveliest big white flowers grew among its pieces. The swallow flew down with Thumbeline and put her on the wide petals of one of these flowers. How surprised she was to see a little man sitting in the middle of the flower! He was as pale and clear as if he were made of glass, and he wore the dearest little gold crown on his head, and had the loveliest bright wings on his shoulders. He was the spirit of the flower, and he himself was no bigger than Thumbeline. There was a little man or woman like him living in every flower, but he was the king of them all.

"Oh, how handsome he is!" Thumbeline whispered to the swallow. As for the little prince, he was quite frightened of the swallow, for the bird was enormous compared to his own small and delicate self. But when he set eyes on Thumbeline he was delighted, for she was the most beautiful girl he had ever seen. So he took the gold crown off his head and put it on hers, and asked her name. Then he asked if she would be his wife and become the queen of all the flowers! Well, this was a nicer sort of husband than the toad's son, or the mole with his black velvet fur coat. So she said yes to the handsome prince.

Then a little lady or a little gentleman came out of every flower, all so pretty that it was a joy to see them. They all brought Thumbeline presents, and the best of all was a pair of lovely wings from a big white fly. The wings were fastened to Thumbeline's back, and now she too could fly from flower to flower. How happy they all were! The swallow sat in his nest and sang for them with all his might. But he was sad at heart, for he loved Thumbeline and never wanted to part with her.

"You must not be called Thumbeline anymore," said the prince of the flowers. "It's an ugly name, and you are so beautiful. We will call you Maia!"

"Good-bye, good-bye!" said the swallow, for it had come to be the season for him to fly away from the warm countries, far away and back again to Denmark. There he had a little nest above the window where the man who tells fairy tales lives. The swallow sang, "Tweet, tweet!" to the man, and that is how we come to know the whole story.

THE TINDERBOX

A soldier came marching down the high road. One, two! One, two! He had his knapsack on his back and a sword at his side, for he had been away fighting in the wars, and now he was going home.

As he went along, he met an old witch on the road. She was very ugly, with a lower lip that hung down to her chest.

"Good evening, soldier!" said she. "What a fine sword you have and what a big knapsack! I see you are a real soldier indeed. Well now, you can have as much money as you want!"

"Thank you kindly, old witch," said the soldier.

"Do you see that big tree?" asked the witch, pointing to a tree growing near the road. "It's hollow inside! Climb up it and you will see the hole. You can get into that hole and right down inside the tree. I'll tie a rope around your waist, and then I can haul you up when you call me!"

"But what am I to do inside the tree?" asked the soldier.

"Fetch the money!" said the witch. "When you reach the bottom of the tree, you will find yourself in a great passage. It is very light, for there are over a hundred lamps burning there. You'll see three doors. You can open them, for the keys are in the locks. Go into the first room, and in the middle of the floor you will see a large chest with a dog sitting on it. He has eyes as big as teacups, but don't let that alarm you. I'll give you my blue-checked apron. Just spread it on the floor, and then you can march up to the dog, put him on the apron, open the chest, and take as much money out of it as you like. The coins in that chest are all copper, but if you would rather have silver, then go into the next room, where you will find a dog with eyes as big as mill wheels. However, don't let that alarm you. Just put him on the apron and take the money! And if you would rather have gold, go into the third room and you can take as much of it as you can carry. The dog sitting on the chest of money in the third room has eyes as big as the Round Tower of Copenhagen. He's a remarkable dog and no mistake! But don't let that alarm you. Just put him on the apron; he won't touch you, and you can take as much gold as you like out of the chest!"

"That sounds like a pretty good notion!" said the soldier. "But what am I to give you in return, old witch? I'm sure you must want something for yourself!"

"No, said the witch, "not a single coin. I just want you to bring me the old tinderbox my grandmother forgot when she was last down there."

"Well, tie the rope around my waist, then!" said the soldier.

"Here it is," said the witch, "and here's my blue-checked apron."

So the soldier climbed the tree and let himself down into the hollow trunk. There he was in the great passage with over a hundred lamps burning, exactly as the witch had said.

He opened the first door—and there sat the dog with eyes as big as teacups, glaring at him.

"Nice doggy!" said the soldier, putting him on the witch's apron. He filled his pockets with all the copper coins he could carry, closed the chest again, put the dog back on top of it, and went into the next room.

My word! There sat the dog with eyes as big as mill wheels.

"Don't you stare at me like that!" said the soldier. "You might do your eyes an injury!" And he put the dog on the witch's apron. When he saw all the silver coins in the chest, he threw away the copper he had taken and filled his pockets and his knapsack with pure silver. Then he went on into the third room. That was an alarming sight and no mistake! The dog in there really did have eyes as big as the Round Tower, and they went around and around in his head like wheels.

"Good evening to you," said the soldier, touching his cap respectfully to the dog, for he had never seen such an animal before. He stood and gaped at him for a while, but then he thought, Well, that's enough of that! And he picked the dog up, put him on the apron, and opened the chest.

Mercy, what a lot of gold it held! Enough to buy the whole of Copenhagen, and the sweetmeat sellers' sugar pigs, enough to buy all the tin soldiers and toy whips and rocking horses in the world. This was wealth indeed!

So the soldier emptied his pockets and knapsack of all the silver coins and filled them with gold instead—his pockets, his knapsack, even his cap and boots, so that he could hardly walk. He had plenty of money now! He put the dog back on the chest, closed the door, and called up through the hollow tree, "You can haul me up, old witch!"

"Have you found the tinderbox?" asked the witch.

"My word!" said the soldier. "I forgot all about it!" So he went back and found it. Then the witch hauled him up, and there he was, standing in the high road again, with his pockets, his boots, his knapsack, and his cap full of money.

"What do you want that tinderbox for?" asked the soldier.

"Mind your own business," said the witch. "You have your money, so hand over the tinderbox!"

"None of that, now!" said the soldier. You tell me what you want the tinderbox for, or I'll draw my sword and cut off your head."

"Won't!" said the witch.

So the soldier cut off her head, and there she lay. He tied up all his money in her apron, slung the bundle over his back, put the tinderbox in his pocket, and marched on to the nearest town.

It was a very fine town, and he went into the grandest inn in the place, hired the best room, and ordered his favorite food, for he had so much money that he was a rich man now.

The servant who cleaned the shoes thought it strange that a rich man should wear such shabby old boots, but the soldier hadn't had time to get any new ones yet. Next day, however, he bought boots and clothes fit for a fine gentleman, and the townsfolk told him all about their town and their king, and what a lovely girl his daughter, the princess, was.

"How can I see her?" asked the soldier.

"Oh, no one can see her!" said the townsfolk. "She lives in a great copper castle surrounded by walls and towers. The king won't let anyone see her but himself, because it has been foretold that she will marry a common soldier, and the king doesn't care for that idea at all."

The soldier thought, I'd like to see her, all the same. But there was no chance he could do that.

Well, the soldier lived a merry life. He went to the theater, he drove out in the king's park, and he also gave a great deal of money to the poor, for he remembered what it was like to be penniless. Now that he was rich and wore fine clothes he made a great many friends. They all said he was a good fellow and a real gentleman. That was the kind of thing the soldier liked to hear!

However, he was spending money every day, but no more money was coming in, so he was soon down to his last two coins. He had to move out of the grand room where he had been living and take a little one up in the attic. He brushed and mended his own boots now, and none of his friends came to see him anymore. There were so many stairs to climb.

One dark evening, when he could not even afford to buy a candle, he remembered that there was a little candle end in the tinderbox he had fetched up for the witch from the hollow tree. He found the tinderbox and the candle end, but as soon as he struck a spark from the flint the door flew open and in came the dog he had seen in the passage below the tree, the dog with eyes as big as teacups. He stopped in front of the soldier.

"What are your orders, master?" said the dog.

"Upon my word!" said the soldier. "This is a remarkable tinderbox if it means I can order anything I want! Fetch me some money!" he said, and the dog was gone in a twinkling. Next moment he was back again, with a great big bag of coins in his mouth. Now the soldier realized what a wonderful tinderbox he had! If he struck the flint once, the dog from the chest of copper coins appeared; if he struck it twice, the dog from the chest of silver came; and if he struck it three times, the dog from the chest of gold coins arrived. So the soldier went back to live in his grand room again, and wore fine clothes, and his friends all remembered him and made a great fuss over him. Well, one day he was thinking, What a pity it is that no one can see the princess! Everyone says she's so beautiful, but what's the good of that if she's always kept shut up in a copper castle surrounded by towers? Can't I find some way to see her? Where's my tinderbox? He struck the flint, and in came the dog with eyes as big as teacups.

"I know it's the middle of the night," said the soldier, "but I would so like to see the princess, just for a moment!"

The dog went straight out of the door, and before the soldier knew it, he was back with the princess riding on him, still fast asleep. She was so pretty that anyone

could see she was a real princess, and the soldier, who was a real soldier, could not help kissing her. The dog took the princess home again. But in the morning, when the king and queen were drinking tea, she told them that she had dreamed a very strange dream that night, about a dog and a soldier. In her dream she rode on the dog's back and the soldier kissed her.

"Dear me, what a story!" said the queen.

And one of the old ladies-in-waiting was told to keep watch by the princess's bedside the next night, to see if it was really a dream or not.

The soldier longed to see the beautiful princess again, and so the dog came for her in the night. He ran as fast as he could, but the old lady-in-waiting put on her boots and followed. She saw the dog go into a large house. I'll be able to tell the place, she thought, and she took a piece of chalk and drew a cross on the door. Then she went home and lay down, and the dog soon brought the princess back. But noticing the cross drawn on the door of the soldier's inn, the dog took a piece of chalk too and drew a cross on every door in town. That was very clever, because now that all the doors had crosses on them the lady-in-waiting couldn't find the right one.

Early in the morning the king, the queen, the old lady-in-waiting, and all the courtiers went to see where the princess had been.

"That's it!" said the king, seeing the first door with a cross on it.

"No, my dear, it's this one!" said the queen, looking at the next door, which also had a cross on it.

"It's this one! No, it's this one!" said everyone. But wherever they looked there were crosses on the doors, so they couldn't tell which one they really wanted.

However, the queen was a very clever woman who could do more than sit in a state carriage. She took her golden scissors, cut up a piece of silk, and made a pretty little bag of it. She filled the bag with finely ground buckwheat, tied it around the princess's waist, and then she snipped a little hole in the bag so that the buckwheat could trickle out all along the way, anywhere the princess went.

The dog came again that night, took the princess on his back, and carried her off to the soldier. He was so much in love with her that he wished he were a prince and could have her for his wife.

But the dog never noticed the buckwheat trickling out all the way from the castle to the place where he jumped up on the wall with the princess and in through the soldier's window. Next morning the king and queen could tell where their daughter had been, and the soldier was arrested and put in prison.

So there he sat. It was dark and dreary, and they told him he was to be hanged the next day. That was not at all amusing, and he had left the tinderbox in his room at the inn.

In the morning, through the iron bars of the little window of his cell, he could see people hurrying out of the town to the place of execution to see him hanged. He heard drums and saw guards marching by.

All the people were going out to see the show. Among the crowd there was a cobbler's apprentice in his leather apron and slippers, running so fast that one of the slippers flew off and fell to the ground near the wall of the prison, where the soldier was peering out through the iron bars.

"Hey, you, cobbler's boy! Don't be in such a hurry," called the soldier. "Nothing's going to happen until I get there! Listen, if you go to the inn where I was staying and fetch me my tinderbox, I'll give you four coins, but you must hurry!"

Well, the cobbler's apprentice wanted to earn four coins, so he ran off to fetch the tinderbox, gave it to the soldier, and then—yes, now we'll see what happened!

A gallows had been set up outside town. It was surrounded by guards and hundreds of thousands of people. The king and the queen were sitting on a grand throne, with the judge and the whole council opposite.

The soldier had already climbed the ladder, but when they were going to put the noose around his neck, he said it was usual for a condemned man to be granted one last wish before he died. He would very much like to smoke a pipe of tobacco, he said, the last pipe he would ever smoke in this world.

The king could hardly refuse him, so the soldier brought out his tinderbox and struck the flint—once, twice, three times. And there were all the dogs: the dog with eyes as big as teacups, the dog with eyes as big as mill wheels, and the dog with eyes as big as the Round Tower of Copenhagen.

"Come along, help me. I don't want to be hanged!" said the soldier, and the dogs raced toward the judge and the council, seizing one man by the leg and another by the nose, and tossed them all so high into the air that when they came down they broke into pieces.

"Leave me alone!" said the king, but the biggest dog seized him and the queen and tossed them up in the air too, after all the others. The guards were terrified, and all the people shouted, "Little soldier, we want you to be our king and marry the beautiful princess!"

So the soldier drove in the king's carriage, and all three dogs pranced in front of it shouting, "Hooray!" and boys whistled on their fingers, and the guards presented arms. The princess came out of her copper castle and became queen, and she liked that very much indeed! The wedding festivities went on for a week, and the dogs sat at the table with the other guests, staring around them with their great big eyes.

THE ROSE TREE
REGIMENT

There was a rose tree standing in the window. Not long ago it had been young and healthy, but now it looked sickly, and had something wrong with it.

There were soldiers billeted on it, eating it all up—men of honor they were, wearing green uniforms.

I talked to one of the soldiers billeted on the rose tree. He was only three days old, but he was already a great-grandfather. Do you know what he said? He told me about himself and all the others living in those quarters, and every word he said was true.

"We are the most remarkable regiment of creatures on earth. In the summer we bear live young, for the weather is good then; we get engaged and then married at once. In the cold weather we lay eggs, and the little ones are nice and cozy. That wisest of creatures, the ant, whom we respect deeply, studies us and knows our worth. The ants do not eat us at once, but take our eggs and put them in the family anthill on the ground floor, stacked layer upon layer, so they can hatch out. Then they put us in a stable, squeeze our hind legs, and milk us until we die. It's a real pleasure, I assure you! They give us the nicest of names; they call us 'sweet little milk cow'! All creatures as intelligent as ants call us by that name, except for humans, and that hurts our feelings and makes us feel bad—can't you write about it, by the way, and show humans their mistake? They look at us in such a stupid way, glaring at us just because we eat rose leaves, while they themselves eat all living creatures and everything green that grows. They give us the most contemptuous name, the most disgusting name; I won't say it! Yuk! It turns my stomach! I just can't say it, or at least not in uniform, and I always wear a uniform.

I was born among rose leaves, I and the whole regiment live on the rose tree, but you could say it lives on in us, for we belong to the higher orders of creatures. Humans don't like us; they come and kill us with soapsuds. What a nasty drink! I think I can smell it now. It's horrible to be washed when you weren't born to be washed!

Humans! Listen, you there, staring at me with that nasty soapy look in your eyes; remember our place in nature and the clever way we can lay eggs and bear live young! We were blessed and told to go forth and multiply. We live on roses, we die

in roses; our whole life is poetry. Don't call us by that disgusting, nasty name—I won't say it, I absolutely will not utter the word! Call us the ant's cows, the rose tree regiment, the little green ones!"

As one of the human race, I stood and looked at the rose tree and the little green ones, the rose tree regiment. I won't mention their name either, or hurt the feelings of any of the citizens of the rose tree, a great family, which can lay eggs and bear live young. As for the soapsuds I was going to throw over them—for I had indeed fetched soapsuds, with evil intent—I will whip them into foam, blow soap bubbles, gaze at their beauty, and there may be a fairy tale in it.

I blew a big, brightly colored bubble, with a silver bead at the bottom of it. My bubble rose, hovered, floated to the door and burst, the door flew open, and there stood Old Mother Fairy Tale herself.

Well, she can tell the story better than I can, the story about—no, I won't say their name—the story about the rose tree regiment!

"Leaf lice!" said Old Mother Fairy Tale. "You should call things by their true names, and even if you don't do so in the usual way, that's what you ought to do in a fairy tale."

THE NAUGHTY BOY

Once upon a time there was an old poet, and a really good old man he was too. One evening, when he was sitting at home, there was a terrible storm outside and the rain poured down in torrents. However, the old poet was warm and comfortable sitting by the fire that burned in his stove, with apples roasting in it.

"Any poor folk out in this storm can't have a dry stitch left on them!" said he, for as I told you, he was a good old man.

"Let me in!" cried a little boy outside. "I'm freezing, and it's so wet!" He was weeping and knocking at the door, while the rain went on pouring down and the wind rattled all the windows.

"Why, the poor little creature!" said the old poet, and he went and opened the door. There stood a little boy, stark naked, with water dripping from his long yellow hair. He was shivering with cold, and if he hadn't been let indoors he would surely have died in that terrible storm.

"You poor child!" said the old poet, taking his hand. "Come along in and I'll get you warm! You shall have wine to drink and roasted apples to eat. What a pretty boy you are!"

And, indeed, so he was. His eyes were bright as stars, and though water was streaming from his yellow hair it curled in a very charming way. He looked like a little cherub, but he was white with cold and trembling all over. He was carrying a nice little bow and arrows. However, the rain had spoiled them, making all the colors of the pretty arrows run.

The old poet sat down by the stove, took the little boy on his lap, dried his hair, warmed his hands between his own, and gave him sweet wine to drink. The little boy soon recovered. His cheeks grew rosy, and he jumped down to the floor and danced around the old poet.

"You're a merry child!" said the old man. "What's your name?"

"My name is Cupid!" said the boy. "Don't you know me? Here's my bow and arrows! You should just see me shoot with them! Look, the storm's cleared up outside and the moon is shining!"

"But your bow is spoiled!" said the old poet.

"What a shame!" said the little boy, picking it up and looking at it. "Oh no, it's dry

again now, and it's not damaged! The string is taut! Let me try it!" And so saying he bent the bow, put an arrow to the string, took aim, and shot the good old poet right in the heart. "There, now you see my bow isn't spoiled!" he said, and he laughed out loudly and ran away.

What a naughty little boy he was, to shoot the old poet who had taken him into his warm room and was so kind to him, giving him good wine to drink and delicious apples to eat!

The good old poet lay on the floor, weeping, for he had been wounded deeply in the heart. "Oh, what a naughty boy Cupid is!" he said. "I'll tell all good children to be on their guard and never play with him, for he will do them great harm!"

And all the good children to whom he told his tale, both girls and boys, were on their guard against that naughty boy Cupid, but he tricked them all the same, for he's a cunning creature! When students come out of lectures, he will walk along beside them in a black gown, with a book under his arm. They don't recognize him, so they link arms with him, taking him for another student, and then he shoots his arrows into their breasts. He is on the watch for girls when they have been to see the priest and when they are in church. He is always chasing people! He sits up in the great chandelier in the theater, shining so brightly that folk think he is one of the lights in it, but they soon discover their mistake. He walks in the king's park and down all the garden paths. Once upon a time he even shot your mother and father in the heart. Just ask them, and see what they say! Yes, Cupid is a naughty boy, and you should have nothing to do with him. He pursues everyone. Why, he once shot an arrow at your old grandmother, but that's a long time ago now. All the same, she has never forgotten it. Shame on you, Cupid! Well, now you will recognize him when you meet him—and you must agree, he is a very naughty boy!

The Swineherd

Once upon a time there was a prince, and he was poor. He had a kingdom: only a little one, but still, it was big enough for him to marry on the strength of it, and he wanted to get married. He was really aiming rather high in daring to ask the emperor's daughter, "Will you have me?" All the same, that is what he did, since his name was known far and wide, and there were hundreds of princesses who would have said yes. But what did the emperor's daughter say? Well, we shall see!

There was a rose tree growing on the grave of the prince's father, and what a beautiful rose tree it was. It flowered only once in five years, and then it bore only one rose, but that rose had so sweet a fragrance that anyone who smelled it forgot all his cares and sorrows. And the prince also had a nightingale that could sing as if its little throat held all the lovely music in the world. He thought he would give the rose and the nightingale to the princess, so they were put into large silver caskets and sent to her. The emperor had the caskets brought before him in the great hall, where the princess and her ladies-in-waiting were playing "Going Visiting." That was all they ever did with their time. When the princess saw the big caskets holding her presents, she clapped her hands for joy.

"I hope there's a little cat inside!" she said. However, what they found was the lovely rose.

"Isn't it nicely made!" said the ladies-in-waiting.

"Nicely?" said the emperor. "It's better than nice, it is beautiful!" But when the princess touched the rose, she could have wept.

"Oh, dear, Papa!" said she. "It isn't artificial after all, it's *real!*"

"Oh, dear!" said all the courtiers. "It's real!"

"Well, let's see what's in the other casket before we lose our tempers," said the emperor. Out came the nightingale. It sang so sweetly that at first they could not say a word against it.

"*Superbe! Charmant!*" remarked the ladies-in-waiting, who all spoke French, and spoke it very badly.

"That bird reminds me of the late empress's musical box!" said one old courtier. "The notes and the way it sings are just the same."

"So they are," said the emperor, and he wept like a little child.

"You can't tell me *that's* real!" said the princess.

"Oh yes, it's a real bird sure enough," said the man who had brought it.

"Then it can fly away!" said the princess, and nothing would persuade her to let the prince come and see her.

But he was not going to lose heart; he smeared his face with dirt, leaving black and brown marks, jammed his hat down on his head, and knocked on the emperor's door.

"Good day, Emperor!" said he. "Can I have a job at the palace?"

"Dear me, there are so many people who want to work here!" said the emperor. "However, let's see—I do need someone to look after the pigs; we have a great many pigs."

So the prince was made court swineherd. He was given a miserable little room near the pigsty, and there he had to stay. He sat and worked all day, and by the time evening came, he had made a nice little pan with bells all around it. As soon as the pan came to the boil, the bells rang out very prettily, playing the old tune:

Oh, my dearest Augustine,
All's lost, lost, lost!

However, the most remarkable thing of all was that when you held your finger in the steam coming from the pan, you could immediately smell what was being cooked on every hearth in town. That was certainly a far cry from the rose!

Along came the princess with all her ladies-in-waiting, and she heard the tune. She stopped and looked pleased; the fact was, she could play "Oh, my dearest Augustine" herself. Indeed, it was the *only* tune she could play, and she played it with one finger at that.

"That's my own tune!" she said. "What a well-educated swineherd he must be! Go in and ask him what his musical instrument costs."

So one of the ladies-in-waiting went in, putting wooden clogs on first.

"What do you want for that pan?" asked the lady-in-waiting.

"Ten kisses from the princess," said the swineherd.

"Mercy on us!" said the lady.

"I can't take less," said the swineherd.

"Well," asked the princess, "what did he say?"

"Oh, dear," said the lady-in-waiting, "I really can't bring myself to tell you, it's so shocking!"

"Then whisper it!" So the lady whispered.

"Good gracious, how rude of him!" said the princess, and she walked away. But she had not gone far before the bells rang out with their pretty tune again:

> *Oh, my dearest Augustine,*
> *All's lost, lost, lost!*

"Go and ask him if he'll take ten kisses from my ladies instead," said the princess.

"No, thank you," said the swineherd. "Ten kisses from the princess, or I keep my pan."

"The impertinence of it!" said the princess. "Oh, well, you must all stand in front of me so nobody can see."

So the ladies-in-waiting stood in front of her and held out the skirts of their dresses, and the swineherd got his ten kisses, and the princess got the pan. What fun the princess and her ladies had! They made the pan boil all evening, and all next day, and they knew what was cooking on every fire in town, from the lord chamberlain's hearth to the cobbler's. The ladies-in-waiting danced about, clapping their hands.

"We know who's having sweet soup and who's having pancakes! We know who's having porridge and who's having cutlets! Isn't that interesting?"

"Very interesting indeed," said the mistress of the royal household.

"But you must keep it secret," said the princess, "because I'm the emperor's daughter!"

"Of course we will," everyone said.

The swineherd, who was really the prince—though they didn't know it and thought he was a real swineherd—did not sit idle all day. He made a rattle. When you swung the rattle around, it played all the waltzes and jigs and polkas that have ever been heard since the world began.

"How delightful!" said the princess as she walked by. "I never heard a better tune! Go in and ask him what that instrument costs—mind you I'm not kissing him again!"

"He wants a hundred kisses from the princess," said the lady who had gone to ask.

"He must be crazy!" said the princess, and she walked away, but before she had gone far she stopped. "Well, one must encourage Art," said she, "and I *am* the emperor's daughter! Tell him I'll give him ten kisses, the same as yesterday, and he can have the rest from my ladies."

"Oh," said the ladies, "we wouldn't like that."

"Nonsense!" said the princess. "If I can kiss him, so can you. Don't forget I pay your wages!"

So the lady-in-waiting had to go and see the swineherd again.

"A hundred kisses from the princess herself," he said, "or we each keep what's our own."

"Stand in front of me," said the princess, so all the ladies-in-waiting stood in front of her, and the swineherd started kissing.

"What's that crowd doing down by the pigsty?" asked the emperor, who had gone out onto his balcony, and he rubbed his eyes and put his spectacles on. "Oh, it's the ladies-in-waiting playing some kind of game. I'll go and see what they're up to!" And he pulled on his slippers, which were trodden down at the heel.

He was in a great hurry!

As soon as he was down in the courtyard, he went along very quietly. The ladies-in-waiting were so busy counting kisses, to make sure it was all fair and the swineherd did not get too many or too few, that they never noticed the emperor. He stood on tiptoe.

"What's all this?" said he, seeing the kissing, and he hit them over the head with his slipper, just as the swineherd was taking his eighty-sixth kiss. "Get out!" said the emperor, really furious, and the princess and the swineherd were both turned out of his empire. So there stood the princess, crying, and the swineherd was angry, and the rain poured down.

"Poor me! I'm so miserable!" said the princess. "If only I'd taken that handsome prince! Oh, how unhappy I am!"

Then the swineherd went behind a tree, wiped the black and brown smears off his face, cast his dirty clothes aside, and came back in his royal robes, looking so fine that the princess bowed down to him.

"Now that I know you, I despise you!" he said. "You wouldn't marry an honest prince, you didn't know the true value of the rose and the nightingale, but you were ready to kiss the swineherd just for a toy! It serves you right."

And he went home to his own kingdom and shut and locked the door. All she could do was stand outside and sing:

> *Oh, my dearest Augustine,*
> *All's lost, lost, lost!*

THE EMPEROR'S NEW CLOTHES

Many years ago there was an emperor who thought fine new clothes were so important that he spent all his money on them. He did not care about his army or going to the theater or hunting in the forest, except as opportunities to show off his new clothes. He had a different suit for every time of day, and while people will often say of a king, "He is in the council chamber," they said of this emperor, "He is in his dressing room."

The great city where he lived was a prosperous place, and many visitors came daily to see it. One day, however, two rascally swindlers arrived in town, pretending to be weavers and claiming to make the most beautiful cloth you can imagine. Not only were the colors and patterns of the cloth amazingly lovely, they said, but clothes made of it had the wonderful property of remaining invisible to anyone who was either unfit for his job or remarkably stupid.

Those must be marvelous clothes indeed, thought the emperor. If I wore them I could find out which people in my lands are unfit for the positions they hold. I could tell who was clever and who was stupid! I must have that cloth made for me at once!

And he gave the two swindlers a great deal of money to begin work. So they set up two looms, and pretended to be working, but, in fact, they were not weaving at all. They said they needed the finest silk and the most precious gold thread, all of which they pocketed themselves, and they worked at their empty looms until late into the night.

I wonder how my cloth is coming along? thought the emperor. He felt slightly alarmed when he remembered that a stupid man, or one unfit for his position, wouldn't be able to see it; he didn't think he need fear for himself, but all the same, he decided to send someone else to see how the work was going.

All the people in town knew about the wonderful powers of the cloth, and they were all eager to find out how clever or how stupid their neighbors were.

I'll send my honest old minister to call on the weavers, thought the emperor. He's the best person to see what the cloth looks like, for he is very clever, and no one could be better fitted for his post!

Well, the good old minister went into the hall where the two swindlers were sitting working at their empty looms. Lord preserve us! thought the old minister, opening his eyes very wide. I can't see anything at all! But he didn't say so.

The two swindlers asked him to be so good as to come closer. Wasn't the pattern very fine, they asked, and weren't the colors beautiful? As they spoke they pointed to the empty loom, and the poor old minister kept staring, but he could see nothing at all, since there was nothing there. Dear me! he thought. Can it be that I'm stupid? I never thought so myself. Well, no one must know of this! Am I unfit for my post? It will never do for me to confess that I can't see the cloth!

"Haven't you anything to say?" asked one of the swindlers, pretending to go on weaving.

"Oh yes, it's very nice! Really splendid!" said the old minister, peering through his glasses. "That pattern! Those colors! Yes, I'll tell the emperor I like it very much indeed!"

"Delighted to hear it!" said the two weavers, and then they told him what the colors were and described the unusual pattern. The old minister listened carefully so that he could tell the emperor all about it, and so he did.

Then the two swindlers asked for more money and more silk and gold thread, saying they needed it for the weaving. They put it all into their own pockets again, and went on weaving at their looms, which were as empty as ever.

Soon the emperor sent another honest officer of state to see how the weaving was getting on, and find out if the cloth would soon be ready. Like the minister before him, the officer of state looked and looked, but as there was nothing on the empty looms, he couldn't see anything either.

"Isn't it a fine piece of cloth?" said the two swindlers, and they pretended to show it to him, describing the beautiful pattern, which wasn't there at all.

I'm sure I'm not stupid, thought the officer of state. So I must be unfit for my job! Well, this is a strange thing, indeed, and I mustn't let anyone know about it! So he praised the cloth he couldn't see, saying how much he liked the fine colors and the beautiful pattern. "Yes, it really is quite exquisite!" he told the emperor.

All the people in town were talking about that wonderful cloth. So now the emperor wanted to see it for himself while it was still on the loom. He called on the cunning swindlers with a very select company of courtiers, including the two good old gentlemen who had been to see the cloth before. The two rascals were weaving away with all their might, although there wasn't a single thread on the loom.

"Isn't it superb?" said the minister and the officer of state. "Oh, Your Majesty, just see that pattern and those colors!" And they pointed to the empty loom, believing that everyone else really could see the cloth.

Goodness me! thought the emperor. I can't see anything at all! This is terrible! Am I stupid? Am I unfit to be emperor? This is the worst thing that could possibly happen to me! However, he said out loud, "Oh yes, it's very beautiful! I like it very much indeed!" And he nodded approvingly at the empty loom. He didn't want to admit that he could see nothing at all.

All the courtiers with him stared and stared too, but they couldn't see any more than the minister and the officer of state. However, they copied the emperor and said, "Really most attractive!" And they advised him to have the wonderful new cloth made into a suit of clothes to wear in the great procession that was soon to take place. The word went from one to another. "Superb!" "Exquisite!" "Excellent!" The courtiers all said how much they liked the cloth, and the emperor gave the two swindlers decorations to wear in their buttonholes and dubbed them Knights of the Loom.

The two rascally swindlers sat up all night before the day of the procession, with sixteen lights burning, and everyone could see how hard they were working to have the emperor's new clothes ready in time. They pretended to be taking the cloth off the looms, they snipped their scissors in empty air, they sewed busily away using needles without any thread. Finally they said, "Look, the clothes are ready!"

The emperor himself arrived, with his most distinguished courtiers, and the two swindlers raised their arms in the air as if they were holding something. "Look, here are the trousers!" they said. "And here's the coat! And here's the cloak! Why," they went on, "it's as light as a cobweb! You might think you were wearing nothing at all, but that's the whole beauty of these clothes!"

"Yes, to be sure!" said all the courtiers, although they still couldn't see anything, because there was nothing to be seen.

"Will Your Imperial Majesty be so gracious as to take your clothes off?" asked the swindlers. "Then we'll dress you in your new ones over there by the big mirror!"

So the emperor took off all his clothes, and the two swindlers pretended to be dressing him in the new ones they were supposed to have made, fitting them around his waist and acting as if they were putting on the train, while the emperor turned and preened in front of the mirror.

"Oh, how fine those clothes are!" said everyone. "What a perfect fit! What a pattern! What colors! That's a splendid suit of clothes indeed!"

"The canopy that is to be carried over Your Majesty in the procession is waiting outside," said the master of ceremonies.

"I'm ready!" said the emperor. "Don't my clothes suit me well?" And he twisted and turned in front of the mirror once more, pretending to be admiring his fine clothes. The chamberlains who were to carry the train fumbled on the floor as if they were picking it up, and then pretended to be carrying it. They were afraid to let anyone notice that they couldn't see a thing.

So the emperor walked in the procession under the fine canopy, and all the people in the streets and standing at the windows cried, "Oh, how wonderful the emperor's new clothes look! What a fine cloak he's wearing over his coat! How well they suit him!" For no one wanted people to think he couldn't see anything. That would have meant he was either stupid or unfit for his job. None of the emperor's other clothes had ever been so greatly admired.

"But the emperor has no clothes on!" said a child.

"Listen to the little innocent!" said the child's father.

But the people began passing what the child had said on to each other.

"The emperor has no clothes on! The child over there says the emperor has no clothes on!"

Finally all the people were shouting, "The emperor has no clothes on!" And the emperor cringed, for he thought in his heart they were right, but he said to himself, "I must hold out until the end of the procession." So he bore himself even more proudly than before, and the chamberlains went on carrying the train that wasn't there at all.

The
Princess
and
the Pea

Once upon a time there was a prince who wanted to marry a princess, but she had to be a real princess. So he went all around the world looking for one, but there was something the matter everywhere. He met plenty of princesses, but he couldn't be sure whether they were real princesses. There was always something not quite right about them. So he came home again, feeling very sad, because he did so want to marry a real princess.

One evening there was a terrible storm, with thunder and lightning, and the rain poured down. It was really dreadful!

Someone came knocking at the great gate, and the old king went to open it.

There was a princess standing outside, but oh, dear, she was in such a state, what with the rain and the terrible storm! Water was dripping from her hair and her clothes, running in at the toes of her shoes and out at the heels again. But she said she was a real princess.

Well, thought the old queen, we'll soon see about that! However, she said nothing but went into the bedroom, took all the bedclothes off, and put a pea on the bedstead. Then she took twenty mattresses and put them on top of the pea, and after that she put twenty eiderdown quilts on top of the mattresses. That was where the princess was to spend the night.

In the morning she was asked how she had slept.

"Oh, very badly!" said the princess. "I could hardly sleep a wink all night! Goodness knows what was in my bed! I was lying on something so hard that I'm black and blue all over. It's really terrible!"

So then they could tell she was a real princess, because she had felt the pea through all twenty mattresses and twenty eiderdown quilts. Only a real princess could be as sensitive as that.

Then the prince married her, for now he knew he had found a real princess, and the pea was put in a museum, where it can be seen to this day, if nobody has taken it.

There, that was a real story!

THE NIGHTINGALE

In China, as of course you know, the emperor is Chinese, and so are all his people. This story happened many years ago, but that makes it all the more worth hearing. Old tales should be told again before they are forgotten.

The emperor had the most magnificent palace in the world, made all of fine porcelain, so expensive and so fragile and delicate that you hardly dared touch it. Out in the garden grew wonderfully beautiful flowers, and the loveliest of all had little silver bells tied to them that rang as you went by, so that you couldn't fail to notice them. Everything in the emperor's garden was so ingeniously laid out, and the garden itself stretched so far, that even the gardener didn't know where it ended. If you went on beyond it you came to a very beautiful wood, with tall trees and deep lakes. This wood went all the way down to the deep blue sea. Great ships could sail right in under its branches, and in the branches, there lived a nightingale who sang so sweetly that even the poor fisherman, busy as he was when he came down to the sea at night to cast his nets, would stop and listen to its song. "Dear God, how beautiful it is!" he said. Then he had to get down to his work, and he forgot the bird, but when he came out the next night and the nightingale sang again, he said the same: "Dear God, how beautiful it is!"

Travelers from every country in the world visited the emperor's city, and marveled at the city itself and the palace and the garden, but when they heard the nightingale, every one of them said, "Ah, that's the best thing of all!"

And when the travelers were home they said what they had seen, and learned men wrote books about the city and the palace and the garden, not forgetting the nightingale: they praised that most of all. And poets wrote wonderful verses about the nightingale who lived in the wood by the deep sea.

The books went all over the world, and at last they came to the emperor too. He sat on his golden seat and read and read, nodding his head again and again with pleasure, for he was delighted with the wonderful descriptions of his city and his palace and his garden. And then he read: "But the nightingale is best of all."

"What's all this?" said the emperor. "Nightingale? I never heard of it. So there is such a bird in my imperial realm, in my own garden, and I haven't heard it? Well, to think what one may learn from books!"

And he summoned his lord-in-waiting, so very grand a gentleman that if anyone of lesser rank so much as spoke to him or asked him a question he simply said, *"P!"* which means nothing at all.

"They say there is a remarkable bird called the nightingale here," said the emperor, "and they say it's the finest thing in all my empire. Why has nobody ever told me about this bird?"

"I never heard of it myself," said the lord-in-waiting. "It's never been presented at court."

"I want it to come and sing for me this evening," said the emperor. "It seems all the world knows what I have here, except me!"

"I never heard of it myself," repeated the lord-in-waiting. "But I'll look for it, and I'll find it."

Where was it to be found, though? The lord-in-waiting ran up and down all the flights of stairs, through great halls, down corridors, and no one he met had ever heard tell of the nightingale. So the lord-in-waiting went back to the emperor and said it must be just a story made up by the people who wrote the books.

"Your Imperial Majesty mustn't believe everything he reads in books; they are full of invention and not to be trusted."

"But the book in which I read it," said the emperor, "was sent to me by the high-and-mighty emperor of Japan, so it must be true. I want to hear the nightingale! It is to come here this evening, and if it doesn't I'll have the whole court thumped in the stomach, right after they've had their supper."

"Tsing-pe!" said the lord-in-waiting, and he went off again and ran up and down the flights of stairs, through the halls and down the corridors, and half the court went with him, not wanting to be thumped in the stomach. They all asked about the remarkable nightingale, known to everyone else in the world but not to the court. At last they found a poor little girl in the kitchen, who said, "The nightingale? Oh yes. I know the nightingale very well, and oh, how it can sing! I'm allowed to take some of the food left over from the table to my poor sick mother in the evenings, and she lives down by the shore, so when I'm on my way back I stop for a rest in the wood and I hear the nightingale sing. It brings tears to my eyes, as if my mother were kissing me."

"Little kitchen maid," said the lord-in-waiting, "I will get you a steady job here in the kitchen and permission to watch the emperor eat his dinner if you can take us to the nightingale, for it is summoned to court this evening."

So half the court went out to the wood where the nightingale used to sing. And as they were going along a cow began to moo. "We've found the nightingale!" said the courtiers.

"What a powerful voice for such a little creature! I've heard it somewhere before."

"No, those are cows," said the little kitchen maid. "We aren't nearly there yet." Then they heard the frogs croaking in the pond.

"Exquisite!" said the imperial palace chaplain. "Now that I hear it, its song is like little church bells."

"No, those are frogs," said the little kitchen maid. "But I think we'll soon hear the nightingale now." And then the nightingale began to sing.

"There it is!" said the little girl. "Listen, listen! It is sitting up there." And she pointed to a small gray bird up in the branches of the trees.

"Can it be true?" said the lord-in-waiting. "I'd never have thought it! It looks like such an ordinary bird. All the color must have drained away from it at the sight of such grand people!"

"Little nightingale," called the kitchen maid, "our gracious emperor wants you to sing for him."

"He's very welcome," said the nightingale, and it sang so beautifully, it was a joy to hear that song.

"Like glass bells!" said the lord-in-waiting. "And see the way its little throat quivers! And to think we never heard it before—what a success it will be at court!"

"Shall I sing for the emperor again?" asked the nightingale, who thought the emperor himself was present.

"My dear, good little nightingale," said the lord-in-waiting. "I am pleased and proud to invite you to a party at court this evening, where you will delight his Imperial Majesty with your lovely song."

"It sounds best out here in the green woods," said the nightingale, but it went along with them willingly enough, on hearing it was the emperor's wish.

What a cleaning and a polishing there was at the palace! The walls and floors, all made of porcelain, shone in the light of thousands of golden lamps. The loveliest of flowers, the chiming ones from the emperor's garden, were placed along the corridor. With all the hurry and bustle, there was such a draft that it made the bells ring out, and you couldn't hear yourself speak.

In the middle of the great hall where the emperor sat they placed a golden perch for the nightingale. The little girl, who now had the official title of Kitchen Maid, was allowed to stand behind the door. The entire court was there, all dressed in their best, and they were all gazing at the little gray bird. The emperor nodded to it.

The nightingale sang so sweetly that tears rose to the emperor's eyes and flowed down his cheeks, and then the nightingale sang yet more beautifully, so that its song went right to the heart. The emperor was so delighted that he said the nightingale was to have his own golden slipper to wear around its neck. But the nightingale thanked him and said it already had its reward.

"I have seen tears in the eyes of the emperor, and what more could I wish for? An emperor's tears have wonderful power; God knows that's reward enough for me." And it sang again in its sweet, lovely voice.

"That's the prettiest thing I ever heard," said the ladies standing by, and they poured water into their mouths and tried to trill when they were spoken to, thinking they would be nightingales too. Even the lackeys and the chambermaids expressed satisfaction, which is saying a good deal, for such folk are the very hardest to please. In short, the nightingale was a great success.

And now it was to stay at court, and have its own cage, and be allowed out twice by day and once by night. Twelve menservants were to go with it, each holding tight to a silken ribbon tied to the bird's leg. Of course, going out like that was no pleasure at all. The whole city was talking of the marvelous bird, and if two friends met one would say, "Night," and the other said, "Gale," and they sighed, and each knew exactly what the other meant. Eleven grocers' children were named after the bird, but not one of them could sing a note.

One day a big parcel came for the emperor, with *Nightingale* written on it.

"Here's a new book about our famous bird," said the emperor. But it wasn't a book, it was a little mechanical toy in a box, an artificial nightingale. It was meant to look like the real one, but it was covered all over with diamonds and rubies and sapphires. As soon as you wound the bird up, it sang one of the real nightingale's songs, and its tail went up and down, all shining with silver and gold. It had a little ribbon around its neck with the words: "The emperor of Japan's nightingale is a poor thing beside the nightingale of the emperor of China."

"How exquisite!" everyone said, and they gave the man who had brought the artificial bird the title of Lord High Nightingale Bringer.

"Now they can sing together. We'll have a duet," said the court.

So sing together they did, but it wasn't quite right, for the real nightingale sang in its own way, and the artificial bird's song worked by means of a cylinder inside it.

"It's not the new bird's fault," said the master of the emperor's music. "It keeps perfect time, and performs in my very own style." So the artificial bird was to sing alone. It was just as great a success as the real bird, and then it was so much prettier to look at! It glittered like jewelry.

It sang the same song thirty-three times, and still it wasn't tired. The court would happily have heard the song again, but the emperor thought it was time for the real nightingale to sing. But where had it gone? No one had noticed it flying out of the open window, out and away, back to its own green wood.

"What's all this?" said the emperor, and all the courtiers said the nightingale was a most ungrateful creature. "But we still have the better bird," they said, and the mechanical nightingale had to sing the same song again, for the thirty-fourth time. It was a difficult song, and the court didn't quite know it by heart yet. The master of the music praised the bird to the skies, and actually stated that it was better than the real nightingale, not just because of its plumage, glittering with so many lovely diamonds, but inside too.

"For you see, my lords, and particularly Your Imperial Majesty, you can never tell just what the real bird is going to sing, but with the artificial bird it's all settled. It will sing like this and it won't sing any other way. You can understand it, you can open it up and see how human minds made it, where the wheels and cylinders lie, how they work and how they all go around."

"My own opinion entirely," said everyone, and the master of the music got permission to show the bird to all the people next Sunday, for the emperor said they should hear it too. And hear it they did, and they were as happy as if they had gotten tipsy on tea, for tea is what the Chinese drink; and they all said, "Ooh!" and pointed their fingers in the air and nodded. However, the poor fisherman who used to listen to the real nightingale said, "It sounds nice enough, and quite like the real bird, but there's something missing, I don't know what."

And the real nightingale was banished from the emperor's domains.

The artificial bird had a place on a silk cushion next to the emperor's bed. All the presents of gold and jewels it had been given lay around it, and it bore the title of Imperial Bedside Singer in Chief, so it took first place on the left side: the emperor thought the side upon which the heart lies was the better one, and even an emperor's heart is on his left. And the master of the music wrote a book, in twenty-five volumes, about the mechanical bird. The book was very long and very learned, and full of hard words in Chinese, so all the people at court pretended to have read it, for fear of looking stupid and being thumped in the stomach.

So it went on for a year. The emperor, the court, and all the other Chinese now knew every little trill of the mechanical bird's song by heart, but they liked it all the better for that. They could join in the song themselves, and they did too. Even the street urchins sang, "Tweet-tweet-tweet, cluck-cluck-cluck-cluck!" and the emperor sang too. How delightful it all was!

One evening, however, as the artificial bird was singing its very best, and the emperor lay in his bed listening, it went *Twang!* and something broke inside it. The wheels whirred around and the music stopped.

The emperor jumped straight out of bed and summoned his own doctor, but there was nothing the doctor could do. So they fetched the watchmaker, and after much talk and much tinkering about with it, he got the bird to work again after a fashion. However, he said it mustn't be made to sing very often, because the little pegs on the cylinders had worn out and there was no way of replacing them without spoiling the tune. This was very sad indeed. They let the mechanical bird sing just once a year, and even that was a strain on it, but the master of the music used to make a

little speech crammed with difficult words, saying the bird was still as good as ever, and so, then, of course it was, just as he said.

Five years passed by, and then the whole country was in great distress, for the people all loved their emperor, and now he was sick and likely to die. A new emperor had already been chosen, and people stood in the street and asked the lord-in-waiting how the old one was.

He only said, "*P!*" and shook his head.

The emperor lay in his great magnificent bed, and he was cold and pale. The whole court thought he was dead already, and the courtiers went off to pay their respects to the new emperor. The lackeys of the bedchamber got together for a gossip, and the maids-in-waiting were having a big coffee party. Cloth was laid down in all the halls and corridors, so that you could hear no footfall, and all was quiet, very quiet. But the emperor was not dead yet. Stiff and pale, he lay in his bed of state, hung with velvet and with heavy golden tassels. There was a window open up above, and moon-light shone in on the emperor and the mechanical nightingale.

The poor emperor could hardly draw breath, and he felt as if something were sitting on his chest. He opened his eyes, and saw that it was Death sitting there. Death was wearing his golden crown, and Death had his imperial golden saber in one hand and his magnificent banner in the other. And strange faces peered out from among the folds of the great velvet hangings of the bed: some were grim and hideous, others blessed and mild. They were the emperor's good deeds and bad deeds all looking at him as Death sat there on his heart.

"Remember this?" they whispered, one by one. "Remember that?" And they reminded him of so many things that the sweat broke out on his forehead.

"No, no! I never knew!" said the emperor. "Music!" he cried. "Music on the great Chinese drum, to keep me from hearing what you say!"

But on they went, and Death kept nodding like a Chinese mandarin at everything they said.

"Music, music!" cried the emperor. "Sing, my little golden bird, oh, sing! I have given you gold and treasure, I myself hung my golden slipper around your neck, so sing for me now, sing!"

But the bird was silent, for there wasn't anyone there to wind it up, and it could not sing without being wound. And Death gazed and gazed at the emperor through his great empty eye sockets, and all was still, all was terribly still.

And at that moment the loveliest of songs was heard coming in through the window. It was the real nightingale sitting in the branches outside. It had heard of the emperor's sickness, and so it had come to sing him a song of hope and comfort. And as it sang, the phantom shapes faded away, the blood flowed faster and faster through the emperor's weak limbs, and Death himself listened and said, "Go on, go on, little nightingale!"

"Yes, if you give me that fine gold saber! Yes, if you give me that gorgeous banner! Yes, if you will give me the emperor's crown!"

So Death gave all those treasures up, each for one of the nightingale's songs, and the nightingale sang on and on. It sang of the quiet churchyard where white roses grow and the air is fragrant with elder flowers, and the fresh grass is wet with the tears of the bereaved. Then Death longed for his own garden again, and he drifted away out of the window like cold white mist.

"Thank you, thank you," said the emperor. "Most blessed of little birds, I know you now! I drove you away from my domains, yet you have sung away all those evil visions from my bed, and driven Death from my heart. How can I reward you?"

"You have rewarded me already," said the nightingale. "I brought tears to your eyes the first time I sang to you, and I will never forget those tears. They are the jewels that rejoice a singer's heart. But you must sleep now, and be fresh and strong when you wake. Now I will sing for you."

The nightingale sang, and the emperor fell asleep into a sweet, gentle, and refreshing slumber.

The sun was shining in on him through the window when he woke, feeling strong and healthy. None of his servants were back, for they all thought he was dead, but the nightingale still sat there singing.

"You must stay with me forever," said the emperor. "You need never sing unless you want to, and I will break the artificial bird into a thousand pieces."

"Don't do that," said the nightingale. "It did the best it could, after all, so you should keep it. I cannot live or nest in a palace; but let me come to you when I feel like it,

and I'll sit on the branch outside your window and sing in the evening, to gladden your heart and fill it with thoughts. I will sing of those who are happy and those who are sad, I will sing of the bad and the good around you. A little singing bird flies far and wide, to the poor fisherman and the peasant's hut, to people very far from you and your court. I love your heart more than I love your crown, yet that crown seems to have something sacred about it. I will come and sing for you, but you must promise me one thing."

"Anything," said the emperor, and he stood there in the imperial robes he had put on again, holding his heavy golden saber to his breast.

"All I ask is that you will not let anyone know you have a little bird who tells you everything; that will be best."

Then the nightingale flew away.

The emperor's servants came in to look at him lying dead, and they stood there amazed.

"Good morning," said the emperor.

THE LITTLE MATCH GIRL

It was bitterly cold; snow was falling, and it was beginning to get dark. This was the last evening of the year, New Year's Eve. A poor little girl was walking through the streets in the cold and the dark. Her head and feet were bare. She had been wearing slippers when she left home, but that did her no good now! They were far too big for her—they were really her mother's slippers, and they were so big that they came off as the little girl hurried over the road to get out of the way of two carriages driving along at high speed. When the carriages had passed, she couldn't find one of the slippers at all, and a boy ran off with the other, saying he would use it for a cradle when he had a child himself.

So now the little girl was walking along with nothing on her feet, which were red and blue with cold. She had some matches in her apron, and she was holding another bundle of matches, but no one had bought any from her all day long. No one had given her a penny. Hungry and chilled to the bone, the poor little thing went on her way, a picture of misery. The snowflakes fell on her long yellow hair. It curled nicely on her neck, but she never gave her own pretty looks a thought. Lights were shining in all the windows, and there was a delicious smell of roast goose in the streets, for this was New Year's Eve. She did think about that.

She sat down in a corner between two houses, one of them standing out farther into the street than the other, and curled her little legs up under her, but now she felt even colder than before. She dared not go home because she had sold no matches, she hadn't earned a penny, and she was afraid her father would beat her. It was cold at home too; the place was only an attic, and although the biggest chinks in the roof were stuffed with straw and rags, the wind still came in. Her little hands were numb with cold. Perhaps the flame of a match would do them good! Dare she take one out of the bundle, strike it on the wall, and warm her fingers? She did; she drew one out, struck it—and oh, how it sparkled and burned! It gave a warm, clear light like a little candle. She cupped her hand around it. What a strange light it was! The little girl felt as if she were sitting by a big iron stove decorated with shiny brass balls and bars, and a lovely warm fire burning in it. She stretched out her feet to get them warm them too—but then the flame went out. The iron stove disappeared, and there she sat with the tiny end of the burned match in her hand.

She struck another match. It burned and shone, and where its light fell the wall seemed to become transparent as a veil, so that she could see into the room inside. There was a table laid with a spotless white cloth, fine china, and a roast goose stuffed with prunes and apples, which smelled delicious. Better still, the goose jumped off its dish, although it had a knife and fork stuck in it, and waddled across the floor toward the little girl. But then the match went out, and there was nothing to be seen but the hard, cold wall.

She struck a third match, and now she was sitting under a beautiful Christmas tree, much bigger and more handsomely decorated than the one she had seen through the rich merchant's glass doors on Christmas Eve. A thousand candles were burning on the green branches, and brightly colored figures such as you see in shop windows looked down on her. The little girl reached both hands out in the air—but then the match went out. The flames of all the Christmas candles burned higher and higher, and she saw that they were bright stars. One of them fell, leaving a fiery trail in the sky behind it.

"Someone is dying," said the little girl, for her old grandmother used to say that when a star falls a soul is going to God. Her grandmother, who was dead now, was the only person who had ever been kind to her.

She struck another match on the wall. It flared up, and in its light she saw her old grandmother herself, bright, shining, and kind. What a welcome sight that was!

"Oh, Grandmother!" called the little girl. "Take me with you! I know you'll go when the match goes out, like the warm stove, the delicious roast goose, and the beautiful big Christmas tree!"

And she hastily struck all the rest of the matches in her bundle to keep her grandmother there. The matches burned with such a light, it was brighter than the day. Her grandmother had never looked so tall and beautiful before. She picked the little girl up in her arms and they flew away in joy and glory, up and up, going to the place where there is no cold or hunger or pain anymore, going to be with God.

The little girl was found in the corner between the two houses in the cold light of dawn. Her cheeks were red and there was a smile on her lips, but she was dead, frozen to death on the last evening of the old year.

The sun of New Year's Day rose over the little body as she sat there with the bundle of burned matches.

"Trying to keep warm," they said. No one knew what beautiful visions she had seen, or how she and her old grandmother had gone away into the glory and joy of the New Year.

Ask your bookseller for these other North-South books
illustrated by LISBETH ZWERGER:

Hans Christian Andersen
THUMBELINE · THE NIGHTINGALE · THE SWINEHERD

L.Frank Baum
THE WIZARD OF OZ

C.Brentano
THE LEGEND OF ROSEPETAL

Lewis Carroll
ALICE IN WONDERLAND

Charles Dickens
A CHRISTMAS CAROL

The Brothers Grimm
HANSEL AND GRETEL · LITTLE RED CAP

Wilhelm Hauff
DWARF NOSE

Heinz Janisch
THE MERRY PRANKS OF TILL EULENSPIEGEL · NOAH'S ARK

Christian Morgenstern
LULLABIES, LYRICS AND GALLOWS SONGS

Edith Nesbit
THE DELIVERERS OF THEIR COUNTRY

Theodor Storm
LITTLE HOBBIN

Oscar Wilde
THE CANTERVILLE GHOST

THE ART OF LISBETH ZWERGER